The Watership Down Treasury

Fiver's Dream

Diane Redmond

A Red Fox Book

Published by Random House Children's Books
20 Vauxhall Bridge Road, London SW1V 2SA

A division of The Random House Group Ltd
London Melbourne Sydney Auckland
Johannesburg and agencies throughout the world

www.watershipdown.net

Illustrations by County Studio, Leicester

1   3   5   7   9   10   8   6   4   2

Printed and bound in Singapore

THE RANDOM HOUSE GROUP Limited Reg. No. 954009

www.randomhouse.co.uk

ISBN 0 0918 6728 2

This story represents scenes from the television series, Watership Down,
which is inspired by Richard Adams' novel of the same name.

The rabbits were on the run. They'd been travelling for days and were tired and hungry.

'I can't go any further,' wailed Pipkin, the smallest of the group. 'I want to go home.'

'We can never go home again,' said Hazel. 'Our warren has been destroyed.'

'So Fiver says!' said Hawkbit. 'But why should we believe him – he's crazy!'

'Fiver has a gift,' said Hazel. 'His dreams tell him what's going to happen. He saw something terrible coming. We had to leave!'

Fiver was sitting alone on a grassy bank. He knew his dream had changed their lives. He also knew there was a safe place where they could build a new warren and start again.

Hazel hopped across and sat beside his brother. 'What can you see, Fiver?' he asked.

Fiver closed his eyes. 'High hills. That's where we must go. That's where we'll find our new home.'

Hazel sighed. He wondered if it was far and if they'd all survive a long and dangerous journey.

'Woof! Woof! Woof!'

The sound of a dog barking made all the rabbits freeze.

Bigwig, a large buck, sniffed the air and swivelled his long ears. 'A dog's found our scent and is coming this way. Run quickly – now!'

The terrified rabbits darted into the thick ferns. The bigger rabbits ran easily, but Fiver and Pipkin were soon out of breath.

Hazel pulled Bigwig aside. 'Unless we distract the dog, the others won't have a chance,' he gasped.

'How?' asked Bigwig.

Hazel looked around. He spotted a hollow log. 'Follow me,' he said. 'Inside that log!'

Seconds later, the dog came bursting through the ferns. When he saw Hazel sitting on the log, he skidded to a halt. 'Grrrr!' he snarled, and charged at the rabbit.

But before the dog reached the log, Hazel ducked inside. A moment later Bigwig appeared at the other end.

The dog looked confused. He barked wildly, and then raced across to Bigwig.

While the rabbits teased him, the dog ran backwards and forwards. Then both rabbits disappeared. The dog was so angry he started to climb *inside* the log. He pushed in his big head and shoulders – and then he got stuck!

The rabbits saw their chance.

'Run!' yelled Hazel.

The dog tried to back out. He kicked wildly with his legs, but he couldn't move. Suddenly the log started to wobble! Then, with a bounce and a bump, it rolled down the bank and smashed into little pieces at the bottom.

Hazel and Bigwig found the other rabbits waiting for them on a river bank.

'Why have you stopped?' asked Bigwig.

'There's no way across!' cried Hawkbit.

Hazel stared at the wide river. 'We'll have to swim,' he said.

Pipkin looked terrified. 'I don't think I can,' he gulped.

The sound of the dog barking made the rabbits sit up.

'Into the river!' yelled Bigwig.

Hawkbit and Dandelion dived in, but Pipkin didn't move.

Fiver turned to Hazel. 'He won't make it!' he said desperately.

'Wait a minute! There *is* another way across!' cried Blackberry. She pointed to a log bobbing at the river's edge. 'Pipkin could float across.'

'That's a brilliant idea!' said Fiver.

Hazel and Bigwig looked confused. 'I'm missing something here,' said Bigwig.

'Quickly! On to the log, Pipkin,' said Fiver.

'I'm scared!' squeaked Pipkin.

Fiver hopped on beside him. 'Don't worry, I'll be with you,' he said.

'Hold tight!' called Blackberry, and pushed the log into the middle of the river, just as the dog came out of the woods.

'Swim!' cried Bigwig.

With a splash the rabbits jumped into the river and paddled hard. The dog didn't follow them – he was afraid of the water.

Dandelion and Hawkbit reached the other side first. They dragged themselves out of the river and collapsed on the bank.

'Safe at last,' breathed Dandelion.

'No, we're not!' said Hawkbit. 'Look! The current's sending Fiver and Pipkin back across the river. They're heading straight for the dog!'

The dog licked his lips as the log drifted towards him.

'What do we do now?' sobbed Pipkin.

'I don't know,' said Fiver. 'I'm sorry it had to end like this.'

Suddenly a loud voice gasped behind them. 'Nothing's ending while I'm around.'

'Bigwig!' yelled Pipkin and Fiver.

'I'm going to push, so hold tight!' he said.

The big rabbit put his nose to the log and turned it away from the waiting dog.

The dog was furious! He sprang forwards to bite Bigwig, but the bank was slippery and he went tumbling into the river!

As the dog splashed about in the water, Bigwig pushed the
log towards the opposite bank. When they were safely there,
Hawkbit and Dandelion helped the big rabbit out of the river.
He was dripping with water and shook it all over them.

Fiver and Pipkin hopped quickly off the log. They looked
at Bigwig with admiration.

'You saved us!' the young rabbits squealed.

'Nothing at all,' said Bigwig, who wasn't used to attention.

'Well done, everybody,' said Hazel. 'Now, come on, let's get moving!'

'But we're exhausted,' complained Hawkbit. 'Can't we rest here, just for a minute?'

'We'll have time to rest when we get where we're going,' said Hazel firmly.

Hawkbit scowled. 'We don't even *know* where we're going,' he grumbled.

Bigwig stamped his foot. 'You heard Hazel. Do as you're told, and hop to it!'

The weary rabbits set off once more on their journey. A long, dangerous journey that they hoped would lead them to the place in Fiver's dream – a safe home in the high hills.

WATERSHIP DOWN

Pipkin Makes
a Friend

The rabbits hopped into the bean field and
quickly took cover under the big, floppy leaves.

'This looks like a safe place to rest,' said Hazel.

'Good – I'm worn out,' groaned Hawkbit.

While the bigger rabbits settled down for
a nap, Pipkin hopped off after a toad.

'Don't go too far,' warned Hazel.

At the edge of the field Pipkin saw a big gull sitting on a fence post. 'Hello,' he said.

'Waah!' squawked the gull. 'You give Kehaar big fright!'

Pipkin giggled. 'Where are you from?' he asked.

'Big water – full of fish,' said Kehaar. 'You know where is big water?' he asked hopefully.

Pipkin shook his head. 'No, we're lost, too.'

'Hungry. Want fish,' wailed the gull, and flew away.

Pipkin hopped back to his friends, who were getting ready to leave. There were dark clouds everywhere and a cold wind was blowing.

'We must go now – before the storm breaks,' urged Hazel.

They carried on until they came to a peat bog.

'We can't cross that!' said Dandelion.

'Well it's not safe to stop here,' said Hazel.

As the rabbits struggled across the bog, sharp thorns stuck to their fur.

'I've had enough,' said Hawkbit. 'We've been looking for Fiver's high hills for days – and now this!'

'I don't think Fiver knows where we're going,' said Dandelion. 'We should go back to the old warren.'

'Nobody's going anywhere,' growled Bigwig, the biggest rabbit in the group. 'Now hop to it.'

They moved on, but Bigwig whispered to Hazel, 'What if Fiver's wrong? We can't keep going on dreams.'

'Why not?' sighed Hazel. 'They're all we have left.'

As evening approached, the rabbits were crossing a moor,
where a light mist had gathered. Fiver was tired and hungry.
He tripped and landed in a puddle, where he sat shivering.
'Come on,' said Hazel. 'The high hills can't be far now.'

'I'm scared there won't be any high hills,' said Fiver.

'Don't say that – you saw them!' Hazel reminded him.

'Yes, in a dream,' said Fiver.

Hazel smiled. 'If we stop believing, we're lost.'

Suddenly Bigwig stopped. 'Hazel,' he gasped, pointing straight ahead. 'Come here!'

The mist had cleared and a shaft of sunlight shone down on a faraway group of hills.

'Fiver!' said Hazel. 'Look! The high hills!'

Fiver gazed at the distant landscape. 'They're real,' he cried. 'Hazel, the hills are real!'

Hawkbit and Dandelion looked on happily.

'You were right, lad,' said Bigwig. 'You were right all along.'

Close by there was a small farm with a barn, paddocks and a vegetable garden.

'Mmm!' said Blackberry. 'I can smell cabbage.'

'I'm starving,' said Hawkbit.

'I could run to the high hills on a belly full of carrots,' laughed Bigwig. 'What are we waiting for?'

'Just a minute,' warned Hazel. 'There may be dogs or cats or Man down there.'

'I don't care – I want some lettuce!' said Dandelion.

'At least wait until dusk,' Hazel suggested. 'It'll be safer.'

Bigwig nodded. 'All right,' he said.

Later, as the rabbits crept into the vegetable garden,
a mouse scampered into the tractor shed.

Kehaar swooped down and landed beside the mouse.
'Hello, Hannah! Want fish!'

Hannah stared at the bird. 'You can't keep stealing
the farm cat's fish,' she said.

The gull squawked sadly. 'Kehaar hungry!'

Hannah sighed. 'Follow me. But this is the last time.'

The cat's bowl was full of sardines.

'Quick, eat!' the mouse whispered. 'The cat's not here.'

But the cat *was* there. She was sitting on the tractor.
Her tail flicked crossly. With a leap, she sprang
through the air and landed on Kehaar. 'Rraw!' she
spat furiously.

When the rabbits heard the cat they ran out of the vegetable garden and bolted across the farmyard.

As they passed the shed, Pipkin ran slap-bang into Hannah.

'Run! Run!' she told him. 'The cat's got Kehaar.'

'Kehaar?' said Pipkin. 'He's my friend, I must help him.' And the young rabbit hopped into the shed.

'Pipkin!' cried Hazel. 'Come back!'

Inside the shed, Kehaar was putting up a brave fight.

'Come on,' he said. 'I not frightened.'

The cat slashed at the gull and drew blood from his wing.

'Caaaw!' Kehaar cried in pain.

Bigwig, Hazel and Hawkbit, who were watching from the entrance of the shed, charged at the cat.

'Yowl!' she howled, as she went flying through the air and landed with a crash underneath a pile of flowerpots.

'Are you badly hurt?' Pipkin asked Kehaar.

'Not bad,' said Kehaar. 'Maybe not fly so good for a while.'

'Then come with us to the high hills,' said Pipkin. 'You'll be safe there.'

'Now hang on a minute,' said Bigwig crossly.

'He's a friend,' Pipkin begged. 'Please.'

Hazel looked at the wounded gull and the tired mouse. 'We're all newcomers here,' he said. 'We need to help each other.' He looked at his friends, who were all nodding.

Slowly, Bigwig nodded his head too. 'All right,' he said. 'Now, let's get going!'

Led by Kehaar, who flew low beside them with Hannah on his back, the rabbits travelled through the night. Finally, at dawn, they reached the foot of the high hills.

'They're big!' gasped Hawkbit, pulling himself up the steep bank.

'We're nearly there,' said Hazel.

After a while, the rabbits reached the top of the hill, where
a soft breeze cooled their hot faces.

Fiver smiled as he gazed around. 'This is the place, Hazel!'
he cried. 'This is where we'll begin again.'

'It's called Watership Down,' said Hannah.

'Watership Down,' whispered Fiver. 'Home.'

WATERSHIP® DOWN

Bigwig Learns a Lesson

The rabbits were settling in on
Watership Down, when one dark night, Holly
arrived. He was scratched and dirty, and looked
very different from the Holly they had known before.
'Fiver's dream was right,' he said. 'Our warren *was*
destroyed. Pimpernel escaped with me.'
He hung his head. 'But we're all that's left.'
'Don't worry,' said Bigwig. 'You're safe now.'

The next morning, Holly was feeling much better. 'I want to go and look for Pimpernel,' he said. 'I left him in a fine big warren that's quite close by.'

Bigwig looked excited. 'A fine warren, you say, I like the idea of that!'

Fiver blinked in surprise. 'What? Surely you'd never leave Watership Down.'

Bigwig nodded. 'It's not much fun up here without a burrow.'

'Well, I don't see why we can't go and look,' said Hazel. 'I'll tell the others.'

Under the beech tree, earth was flying everywhere. Blackberry was halfway down a hole, digging. The other rabbits were eating.

Hazel ran up. 'We're off to find Pimpernel,' he said.

'Good idea!' said Dandelion. 'Can we come, too?'

'It's just Bigwig, Fiver and me this time,' said Hazel. 'Blackberry needs your help here.' And before his friends could argue, he ran off down the slope.

Holly led the rabbits down the hill and through some woods to a clearing, where two fat rabbits were grazing.

'That's Cowslip and Strawberry,' said Holly.

'They look very calm, for rabbits,' said Bigwig.

'Look at those huge burrows!' cried Hazel. 'We'd never build a warren like that – it's far too open.'

'I don't think I like this,' said Fiver. 'It feels bad.'

Bigwig laughed. 'You're always worried, Fiver! It looks very comfortable to me.'

When the fat rabbits saw they had visitors, they rose up onto their back legs and started to dance a slow, strange dance.

'Welcome, welcome. Greetings all!' they sang. 'So very nice of you to call!'

'What's wrong with them?' Hazel whispered to Holly. 'I've never seen rabbits do that before.'

Holly shrugged. 'It's how they greet visitors,' he whispered back. He turned to Cowslip. 'We've come for Pimpernel. Have you seen him?'

But Cowslip ignored his question. 'It's starting to rain,' he said instead. 'Why don't you come inside?'

Cowslip led his guests into a large burrow.

Holly looked around. 'Where's Pimpernel?' he asked again.

But still Cowslip didn't reply. 'Would you like me to show you around?' he asked.

'Yes, please!' said Bigwig happily, and followed Cowslip down a run.

Cowslip showed the rabbits a burrow, with a ceiling made of roots...

…and another that had stones and pieces of glass pressed into the wall.

'What's this?' asked Hazel.

Strawberry laughed. 'It's a shape. We made it.'

Fiver trembled. What kind of rabbits made patterns on their walls?

By evening, Bigwig had settled into Cowslip's warren like he was one of the family.

'This is the life,' he said, tucking into some lettuce. 'A full belly and a warm bed. What more could a rabbit want?'

But Fiver wasn't eating. He sat in a dark corner and watched.

After a while, he hopped over to Bigwig. 'This is a bad
place,' he whispered. 'We must leave!'

'What, now?' cried Bigwig. 'In the rain? Don't be silly.'

'There's terrible danger here!' cried Fiver. 'It's safer
outside with the foxes!' And he fled from the burrow.

The next morning Hazel found Fiver sitting outside. 'What's the matter?' he asked.

'Someone had to stand watch,' said Fiver. 'There's evil all around us. Please, Hazel, let's go home.'

Bigwig called from the entrance of the burrow. 'Hazel, we're off to get food!'

'Come with us, Fiver,' said Hazel.

Fiver started trembling. 'No, it's wrong,' he said. 'The food, this place, those rabbits…'

Bigwig bounded over. 'Is Fiver still moaning?' he asked. 'Well I like it here. In fact, I think I'm going to stay.' And the big rabbit hopped away.

Suddenly a scream filled the air. Hazel raced towards the cries and found Bigwig lying on his side. A silver wire was tight around his neck.

'Help!' Hazel called. 'Bigwig's caught in a trap!'

Fiver rushed across and tried to bite through the wire, but the metal was too hard.

Holly ran to the warren. He asked the fat rabbits for help, but they just stared at the ground.

Cowslip looked at him. 'There is no Bigwig. There never was,' he said.

'You're mad!' cried Holly. 'All of you!' Then he turned and ran.

Hazel was examining the wire. 'Look, Fiver,' he said. 'It's attached to a peg that's stuck in the ground. We can dig it out – like a carrot!'

The rabbits started to dig. When the hole was big enough, Fiver dived down and nibbled the peg until it split in half.

'You're free, Bigwig,' whispered Hazel. 'Come on, get up.'

But the big rabbit's eyes were closed and he lay still.

Strawberry crept up. 'The man will come soon and take him away,' he said. 'Like he did with Pimpernel.'

The rabbits looked shocked.

'What are you saying?' said Holly.

'The man feeds us and protects us,' said Strawberry. 'Then he catches us in his traps. Until that happens, we have an easy time.'

'But that's no life for a rabbit!' said Hazel.

Suddenly, Bigwig moved. 'Ow, my neck hurts,' he groaned.

'You're all right!' said Hazel.

'Yes,' gasped Bigwig. 'But you were right, Fiver, this place isn't. Let's go.'

'Take me with you!' begged Strawberry. 'I don't want to stay here.'

'No,' snarled Bigwig. 'You lied to us.'

Hazel looked at the sad rabbit. 'Yes, come with us,' he said. 'But I warn you, we live a hard life up in the hills.'

The rabbits turned, scampered back through the woods and climbed the long steep hill up to Watership Down. At the top, Hawkbit, Pipkin and Dandelion appeared, covered in dirt and mud.

'I hope you've had a nice time roaming around the countryside while we've been digging!' said Hawkbit.

Bigwig smiled at Hazel. 'Home, sweet home,' he laughed.

WATERSHIP DOWN

Hazel the Brave

The rabbits were inspecting their
new burrows on Watership Down.

'Isn't this the biggest warren you've
ever seen?' said Blackberry proudly.

'It's too big for just us,' said Hazel.
'We need more rabbits to join us.'

'But where do we find new
rabbits?' asked Bigwig.

'Efrafa,' said Hazel. 'I've
sent Kehaar there to have
a look round.'

Efrafa was a dark warren that had been dug deep under the roots of a fallen tree.

Kehaar swooped down and landed on a ledge nearby. He saw General Woundwort standing on a high platform and two frightened rabbits standing in front of him.

Woundwort spoke to the guard.

'What is their crime, Vervain?' he asked.

'They tried to escape,' said Vervain.

'Escape?' Woundwort's eyes flashed in anger. 'All rabbits know they can never leave Efrafa. Take them to the dungeons!'

Kehaar flew back to Watership Down and told Hazel what he'd seen. 'Efrafa no good. Woundwort fierce leader. He punish rabbits if try run away!'

'So there *are* rabbits who would join us,' said Hazel.

'Plenty, but many guards keep watch,' said Kehaar.

'Then we must go to Efrafa and help them escape,' said Hazel. 'I'll take Bigwig and Fiver with me.'

Bigwig and Fiver looked shocked. They didn't like the sound of Efrafa or its leader. But Hazel had made up his mind. They would leave the next day.

At Efrafa, they hid behind some brambles and watched a group of rabbits eating. Kehaar pointed to two of them. 'Those Primrose and Blackavar – they try run away.'

When the rabbits were close enough to hear him, Hazel whispered, 'I've come to help you escape.'

Then Vervain came over. Hazel ducked out of sight, but Fiver stepped on a dry twig, which snapped loudly.

'Who's there?' called Vervain.

Before the guard could find out, Primrose and Blackavar bolted into the woods.

Vervain chased after them and brought them back to the warren.

'Come on, let's go!' said Bigwig.

Hazel shook his head. 'Primrose just saved my life. I'm not leaving without her.'

Suddenly Fiver's whole body began to shake. 'The only way out is to go straight through. If two go in, then out come two.'

'He's having a vision,' said Hazel. 'Two of us must go into Efrafa to get Primrose and Blackavar out.' He turned to Fiver. 'Will you come with me, little brother?'

They stepped out of the brambles and walked up to one of the guards.

'Take me to your leader!' said Hazel.

The astonished guard looked at him, then he led them down a maze of dark tunnels to the dungeon.

As the opening closed, a figure crept out of the shadows.

'Primrose!' cried Hazel.

'So they caught you, anyway,' she sighed.

'Actually, no!' said Hazel. 'We want to be here. We've come to speak to the General.'

'Is he mad?' asked Primrose.

'No,' said Fiver. 'Just very brave.'

Then Vervain appeared. 'The General will see you now,' he said.

The guard took the rabbits to the gathering place at the entrance of the warren.

Woundwort climbed onto his platform. He looked down at Hazel. 'What do you want, Outsider?' he growled.

Hazel came forwards. 'I have two questions to ask,' he said.

Woundwort nodded and Hazel continued. 'Do you prefer peace or war?'

'War!' said the General.

'Do you prefer life or death?'

'Death!' roared the General. 'I have answered your questions. Now you will be punished for your foolishness. Guards, seize them!'

Two guards charged forwards, but just as they were about to strike, Fiver began to tremble. 'Stormhaven is destroyed!' he wailed.

Woundwort looked shocked. 'What are you saying? Stormhaven was my home.'

'I can see a weasel,' moaned Fiver. 'It's coming towards a doe – her name is Laurel.'

'Laurel was my mother!' said Woundwort.

'Laurel pushes young Woundwort away from danger. She faces the weasel. And dies.'

Fiver collapsed on the ground, as his vision ended.

Woundwort was very moved by what he'd heard. He came down from his platform and slowly hopped outside. 'Who is that rabbit?' he asked Hazel. 'How does he know my story?'

'He's a wise rabbit from a great warren,' Hazel answered loudly. 'We have soldiers all around.'

Behind the brambles, Bigwig understood Hazel's message. 'He wants us to pretend to be an army of rabbits,' he told Kehaar. 'Come on. Shake the bushes.'

When the guards saw the brambles moving, they dashed forwards to attack.

'Stop!' Hazel called out. 'You've seen what my brother can do. Harm any of us and your leader will suffer more.'

The guards turned to look at their General, who
just stared at the ground. They didn't know what to do.

'Let the prisoners go,' said Vervain.

Fiver turned and fled, but Hazel stopped to whisper to
Primrose, 'Wait for me, I'll come back for you.' Then he
disappeared through the brambles.

The rabbits raced out of Efrafa with Kehaar flying
high above them. Suddenly the gull let out a screech.
'Run! Run! Woundwort follow.'

The General had recovered from his shock and was angry that Hazel and Fiver had escaped. 'Find them!' he roared.

Woundwort and his guards searched the countryside, but they couldn't find Hazel and his friends.

'I'll get you, Outsider!' Woundwort raged. 'I'll find your warren and destroy your people!'

In the woods below Watership Down Hazel, Bigwig and Fiver heard his voice echo through the treetops. They crouched undercover and waited until everything was quiet. Then, when they were sure the General had gone, they scampered up the hill to home.

'We were lucky to escape,' said Bigwig, as they lay curled up safe and warm with their friends on Watership Down.

Fiver nodded. 'We made an enemy today,' he whispered. 'But you were brave, Hazel.'

'Woundwort doesn't frighten me!' said his big brother. 'I'm going back to Efrafa and soon.'